DECISIONS

DECISIONS

Benjamin Carson High School of Science and Medicine
Tenth Grade Students

Bamba Lo
Abdur Rahman
Teleyona Washington
Eddie Echols
Demetrius Marberry
Deja Hill
Jessica Brown
Mahfuza Meem
Justin Smith
Mahbuba Sumiya

Tasnim Dina
LaTayia Mahoney
Kenneth Long Jr.
Maymana Qaiyum
Wasif Mostafa
Aimia Smith
Alisha Haydar
Khadidiatou Thiam
Shajida Begum
Tisha Islam
Ke'ir Woodfolk

Saif Miah
Jaima Rahman
Catherine Stewart
Shanice Bass
Joshua Hinds
Dasariah Perkins
Sanjida Ahmed
Ta'lasha Hilton
Shelby Parham
Anissa Duynslager

EDITED BY
SHANNON WAITE

Benjamin Carson High School of Science and Medicine
2019

ALSO PUBLISHED BY

Benjamin Carson High School
Of Science and Medicine

A Wider Space
Let Go
Just Be

First Printing: 2019

Typeface Adobe Garamond Pro and
"BBChangeTheWorld" provided by Miss 5th

Benjamin Carson High School of Science and Medicine
571 Mack Avenue
Detroit, MI 48201

www.bchsfreedom.weebly.com

Summary: An anthology of short stories and poems expressing Detroit students' definitions of, and experiences with, freedom.
ISBN: 978-0-359-67351-3

TABLE OF CONTENTS

ACKNOWLEDGMENTS

This book is the product of endless hours of work and community support. These students spent a long period of time grappling with the idea of freedom through the process of reading, watching, and listening to various texts, and then writing their own. There were many people who supported, encouraged, and empowered these students' voices, and who deserve recognition.

A very grateful thank you goes out to…

Susan, from Pages Bookshop, for continuing to help me engage my students by working with us to provide them with an awesome, authentic learning opportunity.

Bob Galardi for his ongoing encouragement and help with making connections to outside resources.

All of the volunteers for helping the students learn that editing and revising are very real and very rewarding processes in writing. These people include: Brooke Harris, Braden Lyford, Bob Galardi, Cheryl Waite, Anlyn Addis, Lamonte Card, Dominic Passmore, Kendrick Youngblood, Lorenzo Harrell, Jamil Allen, and John Martin's AP Literature and Composition students from Brandon High School, including: Shelby, Kylie, Matthew, Joyce, and Jack.

Anlyn Addis and Lamonte Card for their commitment to the community. They offered their experiences to the students regarding very important and relevant topics that encouraged the students to feel a connection between our classroom readings, their own experiences, and the community. This allowed us to have very real, meaningful discussions in the classroom.

Michelle Groven-Nelson for reviewing the writing and Salena Kasha and Isaac Pressgrove for your extra eyes that helped with editing. Two days is not much time at all to edit, organize, format, and publish a whole book, so thank you for your part in cleaning this up.

Charles Todd, Myron Montgomery, Shannan Richardson, Kristen Maher and the entire Benjamin Carson High School of Science and Medicine staff for their continuous and *greatly* appreciated support throughout the entire project. They endlessly work with me to help make the topics the students learn about *real* for them. The staff helps me bring our learning to life. Without their aid, this would not have been possible.

All of the people who continuously support this project through the purchasing of previous years' anthologies and their cheerleading for this year's anthology. Buying these students' books help them understand that their words are important; their voice matters. It gives them a sense of pride and the profits help fund this project for future classes.

Lastly, thank you, the reader, for listening to these students' voices and their stories. We hope that you glean insight from these pages and better understand what freedom looks like to them. We also hope that these insights help you better define your own idea of this topic. This has been an incredible journey on our end and we only hope that it is the same for you on yours.

PREFACE

Shannon Waite

A few years ago, I had some (very old) family VHS tapes transferred to DVDs as a gift for my parents. The process took a few weeks, but when I got them back, I looked over some of them (a few of which were videos of me at the age of one). I watched these videos of my much younger selves and there was something surreal about it. It was me on the screen: singing karaoke on vacation, catching frogs in the summer, and rolling around under the Christmas tree in diapers. I knew that person, but it wasn't *me.* It was a me that I am not anymore. I remember that person, but I am no longer her. With all of the experiences that I've had in my life, I have become someone new, and when watching those videos, I realized: I'm not the same person now as I was back then. I'm different. The same is true for you, reader, and also for all of my students.

A big part of why I've changed is because of the decisions that I've made in my life (and am still making). I have not always been proud of my decisions, but most of the time I have. This means that most of my life has resulted in good consequences. At the beginning of semester two, I asked my students to "cross the line" when the agreed or disagreed with a statement I read off. One of the statements I read to them was "every decision has a consequence." We then had a good discussion on what the word consequence means. After that moment, decisions and their consequences became a reoccurring conversation in the classroom.

You have power. It's probably more power than you think, too. You see, power creates change, but change comes because of choices, and we all make choices. This means that every choice we make, in fact, wields power and when you think about, it's kind of cool to consider how much power comes from just our choices. Our decisions. It's also impactful to think about how often this power comes into play, because we're always making decisions.

Benjamin Carson High School of Science and Medicine's class of 2021 discovered that decisions impact power, but also impact something else: our freedom. They realized this as they spent second semester exploring the question:

What is freedom?

When asked this question at the beginning of the semester, many of the students thought that it was being able to do whatever you wanted or not being in jail. We spent the semester reading, viewing, watching, and listening to various texts. We analyzed them all within this scope, asking ourselves how the characters and people we were learning about were experiencing freedom (or a lack thereof) and slowly the definition of freedom started to change. Our conversations about the characters often came back to their choices and what kinds of consequences their choices had. Why did Steve from the novel *Monster* hang around the people he hung around? Look how it got him in jail. Why did Linda from *Crazy Love* choose to marry the man who maimed her? It kept her in a relationship with a man who hurt her. In both of these situations, and many more that we discussed, their decisions seemed to have negative consequences. Even in the consequences though, we talked about how they still had the opportunity to be free.

Ultimately, consequences have an impact, but our decisions that cause the consequences *and* how we choose to deal with the consequences both seem to be what effects our freedom. Understanding this started to mold many of my students' definitions.

We all face challenges, and we all make decisions in response to them, and these decisions create outcomes. Sometimes we like what comes from our decisions and sometimes we don't; either way, whatever the consequence may be, that's the new reality we live in. With autonomy in this, we are free. We made the decision that may have gotten us in trouble in the first place. Once we're in trouble though, we have the chance to decide how we're going to feel about it and how we're going to deal with it. When we realize the power of our decisions, and how it can impact us and those around us, do we really harness freedom.

After spending lengthy hours reading, watching, thinking, discussing, analyzing, and writing, these Detroit writers are sharing with the community, the public, the world, how they define freedom: your decisions free you. Unfortunately, we sometimes forget that. In these pages, they've shared with you how they see the consequences of some choices, and the celebrations of others, and how, ultimately, both of these paths impact our freedom.

You will begin your own journey down this forested path, twisting through unknown territory as you venture through the lives of these students. You will see the parts of them that help them be and do the things that they want. They are teenagers; they are sons, daughters, brothers, and sisters. They are friends, fighters, Blacks and Whites. They are Muslims, Christians, atheists, girls, boys, gays, survivors. They are more than these words. They have many identities, many communities, and many interests. Here, you bear witness to these as they express what it means to own these different identities, live with the good and bad consequences that come from them, and how those things simultaneously exist in relation to freedom. After considering what they think it means to be free, you can ask yourself: are they free?

I asked the students, based on what we read and wrote, what we should name this book. I think many of the title suggestions did a good job on their own of explaining the messiness of defining freedom. Some of the title suggestions included: Life on Your Own, I Have the Right to Choose, and Breaking Boundaries. One of the students suggested "Depends on You" and this is true. If freedom is created through our decisions, freedom will look different for everyone. These titles show how the students realize the power of their own minds and the roles they play in their own freedom.

Thus, as you read these pieces of writing, you'll see why it's important that we use our power wisely, because you do have power. We all do. I want to encourage you to use power when making decisions so they lead to positive outcomes, but also so you can harness that same power when dealing with negative consequences in your own mind. We all have different experiences and those experiences ultimately lead us to our *decisions.* In those decisions, you can find yourself *free.*

OPPRESSION

Bamba Lo

Taken from home
Loaded on boats
No more places to roam
They came for our throats

Have been owned for decades
Manipulated and used by an unseen hand
Back in the day we were slaves
Off the labor they probably made a grand

To this day
We have been oppressed
We've been led astray
With freedom, we're obsessed

Always running from police
Can't escape because we have cuffs on our feet
This fight doesn't seem to cease
Freedom oh freedom, one day we'll meet

While working, we're digging our graves
That's how it was in our slavery days.

Freedom in no way can be safe. This is because freedom, in the hands of humans, is corrupt and the suppressed will stay suppressed.

- Joshua Hinds

IT'S A LIE

Abdur Rahman

Freedom of religion
Freedom of speech
Freedom of nothing is what it really is.

Roll your pants over the ankle you are gay.
Say Allahu Akbar you're a terrorist.
Is it really freedom or is it just a slogan?

Freedom of religion
Freedom of speech
Freedom of nothing is what it really is.

Wear a scarf around your head you're not welcome anywhere.
Say Allahu Akbar around your friends. You will lose them all.
Is it really freedom or is it just a slogan?

Freedom of religion
Freedom of speech
Freedom of nothing is what it really is.

Freedom is a lie

DO YOU SEE THE FREEDOM?

Teleyona Washington

You might not see what I see, what do you see?
I see no change in this world
I see no peace in this world
I see no chance in this world
What do you think this is Sovereignty?
See we all have Independence but use it differently
Speak it differently, see it differently, have it differently
The laws, rules, limits don't seem like Independence to me
The fear like I'm being trapped
Like I'm not able to have my fun
I don't see the Liberty, what do you see?
FREEDOM is just a word set up as a lion being let out of its cage
Maybe, it is a dark place
Probably, a beautiful place
I know Liberated is living your life being happy with no problems
Time to be free
Independence for me, I see
Maybe, we will be free
Maybe, we're already free
Tell me what do you see?

THE MAN UNDERNEATH THE BEAST

Eddie Echols

To make a man a beast,
yet to only be innocent.

To be defeated and killed with no head start,
to be reminded of what's been forgotten.

To put a label on a man,
Who just wants to make amends.
The name of a beast, a beast that has
No happy ending.

To aim a weapon of death
At the young and kill them off
Bang bang, now they're dead while tears fill the air.

To make a man a beast,
But be the one to kill.

To make a man a beast, a beast that has nothing left in the end

CARNAGE, RIOT, VENDETTA

Demetrius Marberry

"Tears going down my face as if rain was over my head. Cold somehow but I'm in a white room with broken mirrors plastered into the walls. Looking everywhere, all I see is my face broken all over. I feel my blood heating up with fire, so much carnage, so much anger. Then I see a glimpse of things, images, the future."

"Hmm, do you know why you're here, Saint?"

I looked at him through my black shades, not showing my eyes of fear, and smirked a little. His suit was a suede leather suit with a casual western vest jacket slim fit waistcoat. I had to sit up off of the satin couch I was laying on, I had to answer carefully or I was headed back to another mental home.

"No I don't. Why don't you tell me, Doc?"

He was surprised and disappointed. He was expecting a confession of what I did at the mental home. I was wondering how it caught on fire. I know he isn't no regular psychiatrist. He took a deep breath of sarcasm in and said, "You were the sole survivor of your last mental institute after it 'magically' caught fire, and also at your first meet you said that you can unleash a purple flame that you can control, teleport from one place to another, and you can move things with your mind?"

I took off my black shades and put them inside my pocket and showed him the truth. My eyes glimmered bright neon green and I smiled, showing my teeth which were sharper than a razor blade to the touch. I already saw the curiosity and fear in his eyes. I asked him, "Would you like to know my story, Doc?"

He stuttered, "YYYYYYes I wwwwould."

"Well, I ended up like this two years ago. As far as I know, this is how far the mutations go. I ended up like this because of my stupid ego, because of a necklace, because of love. Two years ago I was 18. It was the middle of May and my graduation. I was going to college early, I was top of my class, smarter than any student. My friends Tejon and Justin were suspended from school for the week because they wanted do a senior prank on the principal. I was flat broke with moths coming out of my wallet but I wanted money for a diamond necklace: 1/4 carat with sterling silver. It was gonna cost me 500 dollars.

"The necklace was for a girl I was in love with, whose name is Persephone. Her skin was as soft as fresh picked cotton and a dark caramel color, her hair down to the middle of her back. On that day I talked to her and asked her if she'd like to go on a date the next week. She said with a smile so bright that I had to admire it, "I have been waiting for you to ask me. Of course, I would love to go on a date." After that, I headed to my friend's house for a meet: nothing but weed, drinks and hookah. Tejon was a drinker but couldn't ever get drunk. He always looked sober and could drive better than me when I got high. Justin smoked hookah until his little lungs couldn't take it anymore which was about 24 hours straight. Me, however, I could get higher than the heavens above. My record of backwoods was 9 and still could walk. We all laughing, chilling, we were happy. They were like my brothers after my moms died and my dad refused to have me in his house with his new family. They were my family from then and on."

The Doc looked confused, misconstrued, and said without a doubt "You said were as in past tense"

"Yes, I mean past tense. Now are you gonna interrupt throughout the story?"

"Not really, I'll just listen"

He pulled out a tape recorder, even though no one has a tape recorder in this era anymore. Literally everyone has an iPhone X in their hand.

"I'll just wait to the end and listen again and ask questions at our next session."

"The night was bright. We were loaded, laying on top Tejon's garage listening to Suicideboys. Tejon, Justin, and me were laying there. Then Tejon had to ask, "So where are you gonna get the 500 for Persephone necklace?"

I hurried and got up and asked "How'd you know about that?"

I knew he was on his tenth drink. He responded with a slur, "I read you little diary. I can help you with your money problem. There's this program I did a while back. They pay you to be their lab rat and you write down how you feel. That's how I can get drink and not get that drunk."

I hesitated to responded and asked, "Why haven't you told us this, Tejon?"

He responded, "You never asked" and then he stayed silent.

I thought for a second about how I couldn't do it. If it went down South, I could die. No respawn in five seconds, but actually die. However, I did need the money. I really was in love with that girl for the past 3 years.

Then Tejon interrupted my thoughts and said, "They pay one hundred grand a month. You can get into college."

Justin choked on some smoke and said, "You fat megamind bitch, you owe me twenty-five dollars and you getting one hundred grand a month, where my shovel at?"

My thoughts were changed. *I can do all I want, just one little test, and I can be filthy rich if it goes good. What could go wrong?*

"You could die," Tejon inputted.

"How did you hear me, nigga?"

Tejon looked at me with a straight face and said, "You're that high, nigga. You thinking out loud, like you are yelling, nigga."

I responded quieter, "Oh. Send me that contact."

Tejon said with a clear voice, "Ok."

Justin yelled, "I still wanna know why haven't you paid me and you get hella cash! I swear to Satan, the devil himself, I get my gorilla D'juan on you if you don't pay up my money."

Tejon laughed. "Here you go, nigga," and pulled out a forty and gave it to Justin. The night ended with them sleeping in Tejon's house. I slept on his car.

For some reason I got a text message on my phone and called them on sight, then got in my crappy green beamer car. A woman answered the phone and said, "Hello, thank you for calling Subject Program. Would you like to join?"

I thought, *I have 4 days left for my date with Persephone. I can't wait at this moment at all, I need the money.* I answered with a sigh, "Yes. I would like to join the test subject program. You know, the one where you give money to us for trying a drug or something."

She was quiet for a minute and then she said, "Yes we have a three-day opening for this one spot. Would you like to take it?"

I asked quickly, "Do we get paid up front?"

She said, "Of course you do."

She gave me the address and said clothes would be provided. I drove there and it was just like what I expected: a nice, tall building. They had me in a doctor's office with no shirt, and jean shorts. My fate was sealed at that moment.

I met a man in an all-black uniform with a black lab coat. I was terrified to the point I was gonna run out of the room. Then the man in all black said, "Hello, Saint, my name is Ghost. We are here to make the world better and make humans better. We were made on the foundation of life and to cheat Death himself."

I knew that wasn't his name.

He explained that he was gonna break my mind and reshape it into the perfect human, the perfect apex predator, a riot of full on rage and vendetta in just under three days.

Ghost at that moment asked for my arm and then the test was to begin as soon as the syringe entered my vein and the chemicals took effect. My body was stunned for a moment and then my veins went dark, where you could see them through my skin. I felt so much pressure and power. The guards then entered and picked me up by my arms but I didn't feel anything, as if I was numb. My body was heavy as a boulder. They dragged me into the elevator while Ghost followed them and entered too. He then said, "This unnatural feeling is the first phase of your experimental physical pain. Don't worry. You will feel everything after the paralysis wears off, then we can stop your heart and restart it five times and then we will break your hand, whichever one you choose, and then you have ten straight hours of punching: brass knuckles hitting your stomach by the special ops who are carrying you right now. After that, your body will regain strength and you will be the strongest out of all men in the world. We are just getting started with this experiment, Saint." He then laughed. So did the special ops.

They did as they promised. I threw up after the third time they restart my heart. It felt like I saw God after the fourth, and then it felt dark the fifth time. My body was so hard to move from the pain.

The special ops then took off their equipment. They were shirtless with black pants. The brass knuckles that one of them had said "pity you" on each knuckle. My screams could not be heard. I felt abandoned. The only thing I thought of was what I was gonna wear on my date in two days on Friday. I could feel Persephone's lips touch mine, so soft, so warm, then they smacked me back to reality. I screamed and broke the chains and punched one of the special ops so hard that he laid down and never got up. The other special ops was ready and pulled out wooden sticks. All I could see was red and blood and I had what the doctor said I would have: a riot of rage bursting through my veins. I felt my muscles get bigger and my strength increased at every point of my body. All twenty-five of the special ops ran towards me with the wooden sticks but I could dodge faster and punch harder than ever. My heart kept a low tempo, not even rushing at the moment, and I blinked.

All of the men were down on the floor, a door opened and Ghost was on the other side clapping, mocking me, he said, "Great show. Now look at yourself, you are ripped, man. Abs and muscles, man, you lasted only six hours and, look, all my men down in agony. Now put them out their misery."

I refused and that must've made him mad. He took a gun and shot me. It was a dart that hit me. I felt woozy. He said at my last moment of being awake, "Emotions hold you back. I'll take care of that. You passed the first stage- you're the second one to ever survive."

My dream is so happy. I am in a ball room in a suit with Persephone in a dress, just us, nobody else, and she walked towards me and held my face and kissed me. After that kiss she said, "Wake Up!!!"

I woke quick. My bruises from the other night or day, I lost track of time, were gone. I got up and walked around my room. It was dark but then bright lights came on and I saw that I was in a room with broken mirrors plastered into the walls. All I saw were broken faces of myself. There was a speaker over my head and the doors opened when Ghost came in and said, "Welcome to day two where you will have partial mental pain." He then took my arm and injected a blue liquid into my veins. My hearing became absolute. I was impressed. Then he left the room and then I couldn't even find the doors, they looked like the walls. He spoke over the speaker and said, "This room is designed for you, Saint. Your hearing and sight will increase by the second, but the bright lights will flash on and off, and a high frequency will play and your mind will break. Your enemy will be yourself in this part of this experiment."

The room started to move, my ears felt as if they were bleeding, and my eyes flashed into different colors like a chameleon shifting its shade. I ran in circles because my reflection scared me. Hours passed and all I did was laugh like I just smoked with Justin and Tejon. High off of what though? My sanity, my humanity? Everything was quiet. My eyes flared a neon green and I heard through the walls and punched and punched until I got out laughing harder with my hands bleeding. I saw Ghost. He knew that my mind was somewhere else and he threw me in another room to sleep. I couldn't though. I kept hearing voices that were whispering to kill them all, *then* we could sleep. I felt like floating in the air. Then the cold hard floor, I didn't feel it on my back anymore. I was laying down on nothing, I *was* floating in mid-air. I didn't dream. I felt nothing but pain and madness, carnage, riot of anger, and I just wanted to be next to Persephone. But would she think I was a monster or a hero now?

The night passed quick. without a doubt I knew that this day was my last and about to be my worst. I didn't need to walk. I floated and followed, with my arms crossed and eyes a bright neon green, Ghost gave me some black sunglasses to hide my eyes.

Ghost had something fishy planned, he said, "The last injection won't do nothing but mutate you and give you actual sight, like the into the future, and the ability to jump anywhere in the world and, finally, literal fire power. The way to activate it though is through the sacrifice of loved ones."

I'd be damned. I saw what I saw: Tejon, Justin, and Persephone on their knees with their hands behind their backs tied and Ghost said, "Kill two and one lives. You can go with the one."

He injected a red chemical in me. I cried and walked forward, leaving a trail of tears. Sitting there, Tejon said, "Saint, what did they do to you, man?"

I responded, “They broke me, shattered me, I have no more humanity.” my hands had a fiery feeling but it didn't burn me. I touched Tejon and he turn into ash and dust immediately.

Justin yelled, “Fuck that. I ain’t dying like this,” and jumped and ran and got shot in the back by one of the special ops. I fell down to my knees and cried and yelled out, “No!” I said to Ghost, “I can go now?”

He shook his head no and said, “I said kill two people. You only killed one of them.”

He then looked at Persephone and said, “Finish it. If you want to leave from this bad place, then you have to kill the girl you love.”

Tears went down my face as if rain washed over my head and I saw differently, that I would never be the same. I just wanted to go on my date with Persephone. I just wanted to be normal. Then a voice in my head whispered quietly on repeat *Kill.*

What is my name? I can’t forget my name. Have I gone that deep where I don’t recognize who I am?

Ghost screamed, “Do it. Become the inevitable!”

I screamed. It all happened quick and my mind shattered, seeing dead bodies I caused in front of me. *One more won’t hurt.*

I turned quickly and touched Ghost and smiled while my teeth shifted into a new form. They rearranged into teeth that were sharp to the touch, almost like my whole mouth was fangs. At that moment, I lost it. My name, my mind, my soul, my pride. And yet all I thought about was my date.

I laughed maniacally, craving for my blood and anarchy. Persephone called my name, saying it with tears and fear in her eyes, knowing that what I had become was not man, not monster, not hero, but a god of madness. She said my name one more time and then I snapped back into reality, seeing what I had done.

I laid on my knees and cried out, “Why God, oh, why me?”

Persephone said, “We will be alright Saint, we’ll be ok.”

At that moment, all the people around us were dead in a flash except Persephone and me. Persephone found keys to the handcuffs on the dead body of the special ops guard and got me out of my restraints. Then she picked up the gun and pointed it at me. I took off my sunglasses, my eyes glimmered the bright neon green and I was shocked. I felt betrayed. I told her that we could be together, but the look in her eyes showed that she had more fear of me than a holy woman afraid of God and the Devil.

Persephone said with tears and sniffles, "Saint, you need help or you need to die. No man deserves to have the power of God."

I was out of my mind. I felt in my hand in my pocket and pulled out the magazine with the picture of the diamond necklace I wanted to get her, showed her and said, "I did this for us, Persephone, don't you understand?"

She looked at me and the necklace, lowered the gun, and said, "I'm sorry Saint," and shot the gun at me. I dodged the bullet, but my reflexes were intact and I snapped Persephone's neck.

My mind, heart, and everything was burned. I was officially gone. I made all three of the experiments come true. I passed them all."

The doc looked at me and stopped the recorder, his eyes showing sympathy and pity, like he felt concerned for his life and said, "The bodies, where are they?"

I responded gracefully, "My life is nothing but a shadow of the lives I have taken, Doc. My daily life from that day till now is tragic and dead. I wake up every single day in a cold sweat, screaming, thinking, would I do it all again? Or would I take that bullet and let Persephone live?"

Doc got up from his chair and asked me, "Where are the bodies, Saint?"

I grabbed my black shades from my pocket and put them on my face to hide the tears that I swore I wouldn't shed because I was the one that killed them and damned them to the afterlife.

He yelled "Saint, where are the bodies!"

I got up from the couch and walked towards the door to exit the office. I looked back at the doc with the one lonely teardrop on the left side of my face and said, "Dead men tell no tales, Doc. Saint died when he killed for the first time."

He looked at me with confusion and asked slowly and with cautiousness, "Then who are you?"

I walked back to him, standing in front of his face, and said, "I am Sin," and walked out of the office.

The law gives us freedom.

Actually, no one does. Think about it: even though the law says one thing, people still go and do the opposite. That's the freedom part. Even though the law, or anyone else, might say to do one thing, it'll always be up to that person to do it.

- Dasariah Perkins

THE MISTAKEN BULLETS

Deja Hill

Have you ever lost the most important people in your life before? If not, cherish every moment with them. I never would've thought I'd lose my two boys. This world is wicked, but I know it's just the devil working. It's crazy because I miss my boys every day. It's all my fault. I've failed as a parent.

I dropped out of school when I was seventeen. My parents were divorced and neither of them wanted me. Starting at the age of five, my mom told me that her biggest regret was not aborting me. As far as my dad, he wasn't around much. Drunk dads are normal in my neighborhood. I truly think they loved me though.

I started having unprotected sex at twelve years old. Me and the boys I was messing with couldn't afford condoms. I didn't care though. I just wanted to be loved. I had my first kid named Lamont at eighteen. My baby was a bright, handsome young man. He was blessed with a brother when he was two named Simon. Sad to say, but they are brothers and cousins at the same time. Then, on top of that, both of their fathers were one-night stands. When they found out that they were having sex with the same lady, they both verbally and physically abused me. The hurtful words and bruises still remain with me today.

I live off my forty-five-year-old cousin that used to touch at our aunt's house when I was younger. My aunt was aware of what he was doing to me, but didn't even care enough to address him harassing me, then tell me that it's okay. I've learned to forget and forgive because he was my only help. He treated my kids like his own. He always told them, "You gotta get up, get out, and get something. Don't let the days of your life pass by." I still thank him to this day for telling them that. He also made jokes about my sons, calling them 'Siamese twins'. Boy, were those two always together from their birth until the day they died.

I play the story of my babies' death constantly. The second I found out my sons was dead my life changed for the worse. I told myself I was going to let it go, but I need to hear the story one more time.

I called their friend over to tell me the story again, since he was actually there.

Sometimes I honestly forget this story is about the death of my only children. I even gave it a name, "The Mistaken Bullets." The young man sat down and asked me if I was ready to hear the story. I said yes with a 750 ml bottle of Hennessy to my mouth. He then began shortly after, him staring me in my eyes.

"So, this boy name Jason that worked with your son got into some beef with some niggas on Third Street. The whole hood knew he was boys with Lamont and Simon. The boys on Third Street didn't like Lamont because he was considered the "Marijuana Plug" and they wanted the same connections as him." I rudely interrupted his as he started to begin his next sentence, I asked him since he was good friends with my son, did he know anything about his plugs and connections. He replied no then continued to tell the story.

"Anyway, me and your sons were hooping at the basketball court down the street off Third. I suddenly saw Jason walk up to Lamont with a gun in his left hand. Simon and I was so scared but Lamont wasn't at all. Jason said to Lamont, "Didn't I tell you to tell your boy to report to the trap yesterday?" Lamont looked at him confused and replied. "What are you talking about man? I know that's my mans but what y'all got going on has nothing to do with me." Jason looked at Lamont in his eyes and whispered, "Birds of a feather flock together" and walked away.

"We walked away unbothered. Later on that day the same boy Jason was looking early, ran up behind us asking us if he could hang with us. We all didn't know why we would say no due to the fact that Jason never flexes with guns, and has never pulled a trigger. That small decision is the reason why your boys are dead right now. Five minutes later Jason snuck up behind us and started firing rounds. Two bullets hitting only Simon and Lamont. I ran away fast but I remember seeing them two on the ground with a pool of blood around them.

"Now, ma'am, are we finished?"

"Yeah, we are, but one last thing. You don't think those bullets were meant for my boys, right?"

He turned around looked me in my eyes and said, "I don't know, but I do know, and will never forget, that birds of a feather flock together."

I aggressively opened my front door for him to exit. The whole night after that, I began questioning myself again. I should've finished school, I should've gotten my boys out the hood, I should've raised them correctly.

My deadbeat mother called me for the first time in two years to ask me if I had some money for drugs to give her. I told her that I have money but not to support her unhealthy habit of killing her lungs with smoke. She didn't even mention her grandchildren's death or address the pain in my voice. Ever since that phone call, when I look at myself in the mirror, I see my mom. Although I've never regretted my boys, I feel that I let them go. Another part of me tells me that I should protest against us killing each other. Every ten days it's a story about who got killed in the area. Maybe if our people did things correctly, bad things wouldn't happen. But then I remember that everyone's version of "correctly" is different.

I can't help but think though, if you didn't put them in the world, you sure in the hell don't have the right to take them out.

SHOULD SEXUAL EDUCATION BE TAUGHT IN SCHOOLS?

Jessica Brown

Sexual education should be taught in public schools. Sexual education promotes healthy living and lowers teen issues like unplanned teen pregnancy and STD/I rates. Sexual education would help students learn the good and bad that comes with sex, which would also help students be more self-aware. Sexual education should be comprehensive, not just about sex, promote healthy living, and should have the same curriculum across all schools.

First of all, sex education should be comprehensive. According to "America's Sex Education: How We Are Failing Our Students", "...comprehensive sex Ed "includes age-appropriate, medically accurate information on a broad set of topics related to sexuality including human development, relationships, decision making, abstinence, contraception, and disease prevention"(qtd in "Sexuality Information and Education Council of the United States"). If comprehensive sexual education is age appropriate, that means that elementary school children would learn about anatomy, middle schoolers would learn about contraceptives and STD/Is, while high schoolers would learn about reproductive health, consent and relationships. Medically accurate sexual education guarantees that when students are learning about these topics, they are actually getting the information they need to make informed decisions about their own sexual health without teachers giving biased opinions or myths like abstinence is the only way to not get pregnant or an STD/I. This also ties into the fact that sexual education is not just about sex.

Second, sex education promotes healthy living and decision-making. How does sexual education promote a teenager's healthy living and decision-making? According to "Sexuality Education", "Comprehensive sexual health education helps young people take steps to protect their health, including delaying sex until ready, and using condoms and contraception when they do become sexually active." This means that sex education promotes a better life for those who get it than those who don't receive sex education. Supporting sexual education can help show others the importance of it and fight to make it comprehensive.

Finally, sex education should be taught with the same curriculum across schools. This means that if school boards across the country decide to join together in a conference, there would be an agreement on the topics to teach that applies to every school within the United States. For example, if a curriculum was made for all states, Michigan would have to change its laws so classes were required to teach medically accurate information. With relatively the same curriculum, there is the guarantee that students are getting the sexual education they need to promote healthy decisions related to human sexuality.

In conclusion, sexual education is needed to better teens' lives and guarantee a safer future for them to grow, prosper and learn the proper way to take care of themselves and care for others. Should sexual education be taught in public schools? Yes, because sexual education should be comprehensive, promote healthy living and decision making, and should be taught with the same curriculum across the board. Without comprehensive sex education, unintended birth and STI/D rates will increase within teens.

IMMUNITY

Mahfuza Meem

I stand forth in a time where even
Glass is plastic, where water is wine, and where
The most devoted truths are
Hateful lies…

Immunity?
Repealing conformity,
Avoiding expectations,
Embracing freedom
An endless cycle; a perpetual
Run for something
Which isn't ours?

Legitimate faces are hidden,
Like a tree frog camouflaging to hide from its predator
Even the sun
Refuses to waltz across the sky.
Who wants to be judged?

Limitations are placed,
Over how much immunity we have.
By no one
But ourselves.

Exceptions aren't
Made… besides judgements.
Grace leaves no trace at
The fastest pace.

Humanity... like a twisted fate
But a question I repetitively ask…
Who am I?..

HE *DID* THIS TO US

Justin Smith

I wake up to my alarm blaring the most obnoxious noise. I snatch my phone off of the night stand and press the snooze button. I look at my phone and see the time: 3:47 AM.

Okay… wait, why would I set an alarm for three in the morning? I think to myself. I rub my closed eyes as I sit myself up. I open my eyes and see nothing. Everything is black. I start to feel around but nothing is under me. My bed is gone, my clothes are gone, I try to wrap my arms around my own body, but my own hands go right through me. I open my mouth to scream, but a head just comes out of my mouth. My eyes are wide open as I stare at what is happening to me. The head is turning around to look at me. All I can see is myself staring back at me. I jump up out of my sleep in a cold sweat, confused. I pick up my phone and check the time: 5:45 AM, a half-hour till the time I usually wake up. I throw my head back down against my pillow and think about the weird dream I just had. What does it mean? My mom always told me that dreams were premonitions of things that could possibly happen and my dad told me that they were signs and had a deeper meaning behind each one. I guess I believe both of them. I don't know which one to believe more, so why not believe both?

I force the dream to the back of my head and stop thinking about it. I push my hair out of my face and feel that I am sweating. I get out of my bed and go to my bathroom. I turn on the bathroom light and I stare at myself in the mirror. I rub my eyes aggressively. I must still be sleepy. I wet my towel with cold water and wipe my face off. I brush my teeth and get dressed within five minutes. I turn my room light off and close the door, walking down the hall and knocking on my parents' door. "I'm about to leave for school, love you guys," I shouted. I don't hear a response so I pull my phone out and text them good morning in our family group chat. 6:45 AM. I shove my phone in my pocket and leave for school.

I walk into my first hour class, take my seat, and get my notebook and pen out from my bag. I rub my eyes as I feel myself getting sleepy.

"Good morning, students," Mr. Montgomery says. "Get your materials out and read chapter 8."

I open my book and immediately put my head down. I open my eyes and notice I'm standing up, holding a geometry book that is covered with blood. Everybody in the class is staring at me. A student, Megan, is laying down in front of me with fear in her eyes, tears rolling down her cheeks, and blood on her face. I lower the book as security enters the classroom. They escort me to the principal's office.

I sit outside of Mr. Sharp's office for about thirty minutes as students from my class are being called in as eyewitnesses.

"Kamon, come in here," he says as the last student leaves his office. "What's gotten into you?" Mr. Sharp asks.

"I- I don't know what happened sir," I reply.

He begins to raise his voice, "You assaulted a young lady with a book and caused internal bleeding! Tell me what happened now, boy, or there are going to be serious consequences. Even though the consequences are already serious enough."

"I swear I don't know what happened. All I remember doing is laying my head down to take a nap one minute, then the next minute I was standing up in front of Megan holding a book."

"Her mother wants to press charges, which means you might go to jail," he replies. "Kamon, you're going to have to find another school to attend."

"What does that mean?" I question.

"You're expelled," he says.

I feel my heart sink to the pit of my stomach. The school year is almost over. What school am I going to find in May that's still accepting students? What am I going to do?

"Kamon. Kamon!" Mr. Sharp yells.

I look up as Mr. Sharp's loud voice pulls me from my deep thoughts.

"You're excused," he says.

I walk out of his office and I feel my phone vibrate. I pull it out and see it's a text message from Anton, my classmate.

Are you okay?

Yeah man. I don't know what happened.

U lost it man. You jumped out of your seat and hit Megan in the back of her head with a book.

I don't remember doing any of that. All I remember is laying my head down at the start of class, then I open my eyes to Megan on the floor in front of me

I put my phone back in my pocket as I try to think about what happened. I can't remember a thing. Mr. Sharp steps out of his office and says, "Go get your stuff. Your mom is on her way to come pick you up." I walk towards my locker to go get my jacket. Ten minutes later, the principal tells me that my mom is outside and that I'm released.

I stare out the window as the school seems to get smaller the farther we get from it. I try to remember what happened at school. Nothing. I can't even remember the school day. The last thing I can remember is walking towards the bus stop this morning.

We arrive home. It's 12:35 PM. I start to feel hungry. *Did I eat anything today?* I ask myself. I go to make myself some food. I look in the fridge and decide to make a sandwich, grabbing the bread, mayo, cheese, ham, plate, and knife.

I blink rapidly as I feel a sharp pain on my forearm. I look down and I find myself dragging the knife across my arm. I throw the knife down on the stone, tile floor and see blood splattered everywhere. I scream out in pain as I grab my arm in an attempt to stop too much blood from coming out. I hear heavy, fast footsteps coming from my mom's room. As she enters the kitchen, her eyes are full of fear as she takes in the scenery.

"Oh my God," she exclaims, "What happened?"

"I don't know," I say through gritted teeth. "I was making a sandwich and then I was cutting my arm. Mom, I don't know what's happening to me," I say with tears rolling down my face.

"Get in the car. Now!" My mom shouts as she's reaching for her car keys. My arm is still bleeding, everything is going dark. I try to keep my eyes open, but they're too heavy. I feel myself drifting off. Everything is black.

I'm sitting in the waiting room as my mother is talking to the therapist. Every time I look at the receptionist, her head quickly turns away from me with a worried look on her face. After waiting for about ten minutes, my mother and the therapist finally emerge. I search my mother's face for an expression, but nothing is there.

"Son, you have Dissociative Identity Disorder, or DID," The therapist starts.

"What's that?" I ask.

"Kamon, you have multiple personalities," my mom replies.

"Is that why I black out and can't remember things?" I ask.

"Amnesia and migraines are common effects of DID. Sometimes, the person diagnosed with it has amnesia so bad that they can't remember if they ate breakfast or not," the therapist says. My mom and the therapist begin talking about the medicine that I can take for my migraines. They finish talking and we go home.

As soon as we arrive home, my mom gives me the medication for my migraines and I go up to my room. I feel a little sleepy as I'm walking up the stairs. I flop down on my bed and close my eyes immediately.

I wake up with a pen and my notebook in my hand. I look down at the notebook and it's open to a page. As my eyesight is focusing, I notice there's something written on the page that's not my handwriting.

"Hi, I'm Kevin. The 'other half' of you." I stare at the page in awe, in a state of confusion. Can I communicate with it now? Or should I say "him" now? Maybe I can tell him what he can and can't do. Does he have my memories? I decide to write down a list of specific things that he needs to know, questions that need to be answered, and figure out why and how this happened.

I start to feel better knowing that I have some control over what's different about me now. I think about how maybe Kevin doesn't understand right from wrong since he's not an "actual person." Maybe I can help him.

Freedom is being able to use our own freewill to make decisions, choose our own future, and to say or hear whatever we want. Freedom is a life of possibilities and opportunities and the faith that life will be successful. It stands for something greater than just the right to act however we choose. Freedom is a safe place. When you want, you can go anywhere.

- Sanjida Ahmed

THE BREEZE

Mahbuba Sumiya

Maybe the world doesn't see the true light,
Maybe I am not who I think I am.
All my life, played to catch every star.
All my life, played to live fearless.
All my life, played not to be ashamed of my identity.

Now, I'm afraid.
I'm afraid to be judged.
I'm afraid of my decision.
I'm afraid of expressing my religious identity.

Maybe it's time to stand.
Maybe it's time to fight for my dreams.
There's nothing so painful as an unpublished vision.
I am shattering every time I see that wild smile.
Sanity is a lie.

I can't decide to swallow my identity or the words.
Spontaneous eyes make me feel curious.
While smiles and curtains hide my little lie.

Wake up world.
Wake up to accept me.
Wake up to protect me from that bullet.
Wake up to glow the world with the essence of diversity.

BOUND

Tasnim Dina

A white dove that is caged with wings that are clipped,
A life that is lived with happiness stripped.
Unsaid feelings that are true but are always disguising,
Surrounded by people who are constantly downsizing.

We live in a society where true faces can never be shown,
Wearing a mask that we make for our very own.
Living in a country where we're told what to do,
Never given enough or allowed to choose.

Religion keeps me bound like a dog on a leash,
Always expected to have a modest appearance and prestige.
Forced to live up to goals that I will never reach,
Watching others live their lives without boundaries.

The prospect of change causes me great fear,
As I watch life go by in high gear.
My eyes are kaleidoscopes as I shed a tear,
Hoping the day I'll become free is near.

BEING DIFFERENT IS DIFFICULT

LaTayia Mahoney

I didn't expect this to happen. They told me I was going to be broken forever. I'm trying to keep it together but nothing is working for me. I hate being different. No one cares or appreciates the fact that I'm human just like them. I tried to speak about my problems, but I don't have friends or family that I can talk to. Even if I did, they wouldn't be able to fix my problems like I want them to.

All my life I felt different. I had no one, and when I did, no one cared. They thought I was crazy and had mental issues. I can admit I'm a bit sick, but that's not the point. I tried to say what was on my mind to the therapist, but I was scared and afraid to be open about it. Besides, it's not like he was going to listen anyway. He was too busy flirting with the receptionist at the front desk. Why do I have to go through this? Why couldn't it be someone else?

I'm trying not to listen to the thoughts in my head, but I have to release this pain. I told my mom, but she thinks it's a phase and I'll get over it. She suggested that I move in with my grandparents. I asked her why and she told me that she couldn't deal with my nonsense anymore. She thinks I'm an embarrassment to the world. It hurts to hear that from my own mother. I didn't want to tell my mother I was relieved, but deep down I knew she was relieved too.

"Hola abuela"

"Hola, mi querido nieta. ¿Cómo estás?"

I started crying before I answered. I knew when I told my grandmother everything, she was going to be speechless.

"Es mucho lo que quiero decirte pero..." I paused and took deep breaths. "Grandmother, I'm sick and broken. Rolling around in this wheelchair with a broken arm is useless for me. I can't stand being alone anymore. I tried asking for help but no one listened. Even the lady you raised, also known as my mother." Before I could finish, she grabbed me, hugged me and gave me a kiss and told me she would always love me no matter what was going on. I would always be loved by her.

"Abuela, sólo quiero ser libre. Libre como ellos," I said with a smile.

She paused with a confused, disappointed look on her face. I wanted to tell Grandmother that I was paralyzed and won't be able to walk anymore but her optimistic assumptions sounded better than the truth. I hated lying to her. I felt like it would make things worse. I just didn't want her to not love me anymore. She looked at me with tears in her eyes and said I can be free to do anything no matter how hard life hit me. She suggested I see a professional. Someone who she knows would listen and help me fix my problems. I know Grandmother isn't able to fix all my problems but I know she's able to fix my broken heart.

I asked Grandmother, "Why the confused and disappointed look?" She didn't answer but I know it's because of my mother. Back then, before she became a mother, she was a bright woman and was always on top of her game, but now she's falling apart.

"Jazmine."

"Is there a Jazmine Lopez here?"

"Estoy aquí."

I had mixed feelings about this therapy session. I felt like she was not going to listen but it was worth a try. As we sat down, before Kathy could talk, I started pouring my heart out. I knew it was too much for her to handle but seeing the expression on her face made me realize she was actually listening. I started to tell Kathy about the car crash but I burst into tears. Losing the feeling in my legs was hard, but losing the ability to do things on my own was even harder.

We talked for hours. I started to question her thinking she wasn't listening. She started to respond in ways I didn't know she would. I couldn't quite understand what she was saying because I was shocked at the fact that she was actually listening to me.

She stopped and ask what was wrong because of the puzzled look on my face.

I turned to her and smiled and said, "You're listening to me. You are really listening to me." I shed a tear, a tear of joy. She smiled with excitement.

I had to ask why she wanted to help me but before she could answer I felt a small shake in my legs. I'd never felt that before. After the accident, I always thought I would be like this forever. Well, at least that's what I was told. I looked at Ms. Kathy and she said it could be a sign.

I didn't know before that Grandmother and Ms. Kathy were friends. Grandmother always told me she had a problem fixer, but never told me her name. It seemed like their bond had grown stronger. A week went by and they talked more than usual. A few months later, Grandmother and Ms. Kathy burst in with exciting news. They told me I was going to be able to walk again.

"Abuela, ¿eso significa que puedo ser libre?"

"Sí, libre de hacer cualquier cosa."

I wanted to cry but I knew this day would come. I didn't get too happy though because when I do, there is always something bad that happens.

As the weeks went by, I began to develop stronger feeling and muscle in my legs. I practiced standing every once in a while, just to get used to standing.

"¡Voy a poder caminar!"

She stopped with a frightened look on her face. I was a bit worried. I hoped it wasn't bad news.

"Abuela, ¿qué pasa?"

"Jazmine mi amor, es tu madre, ella quiere verte."

I couldn't believe it. She sent me away because she didn't want to deal with me but that after all that time, she wanted to see me. I couldn't stand looking at my mother in the eyes. I wanted to ask her why but I could just imagine the excuses she would make.

"I'm glad you decided to talk."

"There's nothing to talk about."

"Jazmine, I'm your mother and I do care about you."

"If you cared you wouldn't have sent me away."

"I sent you away to give you a better life"

"No, you sent me away because you didn't care. You know the things you say hurt me and to be honest, I was relieved when I left home. I feel more free here with Grandmother."

She froze with a shocked look on her face. I was angry. I had no choice but to release the pain. She had to hear what I had to say. I wanted to make sure she heard me. The things she said hurt me but I couldn't hold a grudge on her forever. I know she's my mother but she had to understand that I have pain too and the world doesn't revolve around her.

As I spoke my words, she shed a tear. Usually when I speak to her she turns away, but this time she actually listened. In my mind, I never thought this would happen. It warmed my heart.

"I never thought you felt this way. I just wanted you to have a life, one like I never had."

"Mother, I would have understood if you would've just told me."

"I didn't know how to tell you."

"My life wasn't as easy as I made it seem."

"Well I want our relationship to be stronger than what it is."

She smiled with excitement. Knowing she was going to do better meant that our journey would continue.

I always wanted our bond to get stronger. I never knew that me talking to her would change her. She always told me I would have a voice. A voice that could change people. I knew I had the courage, but I never knew how to use it.

Eight months later, I'm able to walk by myself. Physical therapy really helped me get through my physical challenges. My mother and I now have a relationship stronger than ever. I always wanted to tell my Abuela that I was going to be paralyzed before, but she told me she'd always known what happened to me, she just wanted me to build the courage to tell her myself.

BABY BIRD

Kenneth Long Jr.

Baby bird wants to fly away
Shielded by its mother
Dreams to fly away like an eagle
Shedding its feathers like wasted dreams
Each feather falling deeper into despair
Never to be seen again

Smile when its mother's around
Afraid to do otherwise
Wants to fly
Fly and float
Further and further away
Never to be afraid again
But fears what its mother would do
Never tasting the sky for himself
Left alone to wither away

FREE BIRD

Maymana Qaiyum

You set me free
Now I fly and fly and fly
Over the same field
Yet there is no honey to suck
All the flowers look the same
They are all empty.

I am free now but my wings
Know only about the place
Where they opened
For the first time.

I will fly, float and run
I will sing when I roam;

Then I will come back home.

FREE TUITION FOR THE PEOPLE

Wasif Mostafa

Nowadays, people need a college degree to get a somewhat respectable job. There are many people in the U.S. who are more than capable of making it and performing well in college. Even though they are capable enough, they do not go to college because they cannot afford the fees. They should be able to go to college for free and their acceptance should be based entirely on merit. Giving these students free college tuition would also help them in the future. Students who averaged a GPA of 3.5 or above and managed to stay on honor roll throughout all of high school should be able to get free tuition in college.

First of all, free college tuition would allow the students to focus more on their education and themselves. This claim is supported by "Should College Be Free? Here's What You Need to Consider" where it states, "Students would be able to focus more on their studies rather than worrying about how to scrape together enough funds for each upcoming school term. As a result, more of them might graduate on time, ready to take on important jobs in their communities." Not having to worry about college fees would allow the students to completely focus on their education and not add extra stress. The students could also have more time to themselves and allow their minds to rest as they don't have to work jobs to stay at the college. Some people might say that not having to worry about college fees would make the students carefree. That statement isn't accurate because the students still have to manage their lifestyle and their responsibilities. Everyone that gets accepted into a college has already earned their spot and shouldn't have to worry about how they'll manage to stay there because they can't afford the fees.

Secondly, making colleges free would allow there to be more equality between the students regardless of their financial situation. In the article "Should College Be Free? Here's What You Need to Consider" it says, "Many of America's top-performing high school students never apply to the most challenging colleges and universities even though they have the ability to succeed at them. They often come from minority and low-income households and end up pursuing more affordable, less-selective schools instead. And that helps create a widening gap between wealthier families and those that are less affluent." Having free tuition gives an equal chance to everyone and helps those who are less fortunate. This allows for merit to shine and lets the people who are less financially-able to have more opportunities. Some might say that everyone getting a degree might decrease the value of a college degree but doing so only levels the playing field and, as mentioned before, offers merit to shine.

Lastly, free tuition allows students to graduate without student loan debt. That would allow the students to leave college behind after they graduate and start their lives without financial issues. The article "Why Should Colleges Be Free? Pros and Cons of Tuition-Free College" states, "Without the weight of student loan debt, more college graduates might buy houses rather than renting apartments. They might buy cars, spend more on healthy food, travel more: In essence, they could contribute more to the economy." Graduating without being in debt would allow them to rest their mind after finishing college and wouldn't put them under financial pressure right away. Some people, mainly corporations, might support student loans but student loans never help students and end up having a negative effect on the mindset of the students. Students need a fresh start after college and being in debt doesn't allow that to happen.

There are people who think college tuition shouldn't be free because they think it would lead to some people losing value of degrees or would put colleges or the under a financial dilemma. There is a possibility of it happening but schools could avoid accepting too many students by vetting them thoroughly and accepting the ones who deserve to be there. As for degrees losing value, the people who have earned them worked hard and it will surely be recognized. Making college tuition free is a good way to help the students and the community.

In conclusion, college tuition should be free. Not having to worry about college fees lets students focus on themselves and their education at school. It also allows for more people to get the education that they desire and ends up providing more opportunities for people who would otherwise be limited in choosing their career pathway. Not having to worry about student loan after graduation would allow students to start their lives without any pressure and gives them time to figure their lives out. The idea of free college isn't a perfect one and it would be hard to create a perfect system for it but, in the end, free college tuition would end up helping a lot of people and especially the ones who deserve it.

Freedom is a choice. It depends on the individual and what choices he or she makes all throughout his or her life. Freedom may not be the same for everyone, but it is given to everyone. Our choices and decisions may define what freedom we receive.

- Mahbuba Sumiya

INSIDE VS OUTSIDE

Aimia Smith

It is your choice to pick
Either being held in captivity
Or living a normal life
To be held inside from everyone
Or released into the open
A chance to be blessed
Or a chance to be cursed
To go off into the world with success
Not dissatisfaction and regret
Having to lose your choice and action
To having total control of choice
Not taking chances
To risking your life
Staying inside the box
Or going outside
You choose what your life should be

APRIL 12TH

Alisha Haydar

Sarah was walking along the side of the road, taking in the sweet air and the sight of the dancing dandelions. She hadn't been outside in what seemed like ages. She was walking along the train tracks now, cars zooming past her as she pranced about. She inhaled deeply.

"I can breathe!' she shouted into the wind.

It happened about five months ago, the incident that would change Sarah Yameen's life, and not for the better. Sarah was at her local middle school, playing the sport she loved so much, soccer. She was exceptional at the game, ranked in the top five in her district. Her school's team had made it to the nationals and was playing with other talented and very competitive teams. Not only were there middle school teams, there were also high school teams which made the competition even more difficult.

After multiple rounds and games, Sarah's team was the only middle school that had made it to the championship round. Now it was just her team and three other high school teams. The middle school team had to go up against and beat two other teams in order to take home the gold. Thankfully, they had made it past the first high school team and now all that was left was to keep scoring until they dropped against the second. Sarah was the goalie this round since she had been running around the most throughout the games.

Sarah had a keen talent for soccer no matter what position she played. She was good at both offense and defense when it came to her favorite sport. She could block any kick thrown at her at any force and at any speed, however, she was nervous this time around since she was playing against older kids. She tried to imagine some plays in her head to boost her confidence.

It worked and she went to take her position at the goal. The game had begun and her teammates were running around making as many goals as they possibly could and Sarah also blocked as many goals as she possibly could, however, there was this one kicker that was too good, even for Sarah Yameen. Every goal that he attempted to make went in with ease.

"I need to step up my game," Sarah whispered to herself. "We don't have much time left and we're tied."

Then, out of nowhere, the soccer ball came rushing at her in lightning fast speed. Before Sarah knew what hit her, she was passed out on the soccer field surrounded by members of both of the teams and their designated coaches. The next day, Sarah awoke from her slumber which seemed to have lasted for days to her family.

"Where am I?" Sarah queried worriedly. Then she jumped up from her hospital bed and shouted, "The game!"

Sarah saw a doctor and her sister, Miranda Yameen, who hurried to her side. "Shh, shh, it's okay."

"But the championships, Meer, what about the game?"

"It's over and done with, the last game was postponed because of your injury, we're playing again next month."

"My injury?"

"The ball flew at you and you weren't able to dodge. It knocked you out. The doctors said that you had a concussion and some internal bleeding. I'm sorry, Sarah, but it caused a lot of damage to your brain."

"I'll still be able to play though, right?"

Miranda looked down at her feet in regret and her doctor spoke up, "I'm sorry Sarah," the doctor said. "You will be immobile for at least three months until you've fully recovered. You have a TBI, a traumatic brain injury. The brain injury caused a malfunction of sorts in your nerves and your brain isn't able to process movements normally anymore. There's a defect in your cognitive abilities so it will be difficult for you to comprehend information or organize it. You won't be able to play or do much of anything else for a long time."

Sarah was in utter disbelief. She had been playing soccer all her life and it was the one thing that gave her life. Now, it was the one thing that was taking her life away from her. The doctor told her more details, like how Sarah would have to stay in the hospital throughout those three months for proper monitoring and physical rehabilitation. The days went by very slowly for Sarah, the seconds felt like centuries to her. She felt as though her life was slipping away from her fingers. Sarah would watch soccer matches on the hospital television in her room and look at Miranda expectantly, as if to hear about the team's progress. Miranda never uttered a word to Sarah.

"How are the games going, Meer? Isn't the rematch coming up soon?" questioned Sarah.

"Uh, yeah. I have to go Sarah, it's getting pretty late."

"Oh, okay. Bye, Meer. Be safe."

Three days had passed and Miranda hadn't come to visit Sarah yet. She wondered to herself, *Is there something she isn't telling me? It must be serious if she keeps avoiding me like this.* Sarah texted Miranda and asked her to come visit her the next day. She said she had something important to ask her. Miranda agreed and said she also had something important to tell Sarah as well.

The next day, Miranda came to the hospital and sat beside Sarah's head as she usually did. She tucked Sarah in and helped her get comfortable. "Sarah, there's something I really need to tell you. It's your second month here and I don't think it's right to keep it from you. The rematch happened and our team lost."

"Is that why you've been avoiding me? It's okay you know, losses happen. That doesn't mean you beat yourself up about it."

"There's something else too, Sarah. Listen to me carefully, please. After the first day you were admitted into the hospital, I talked to your doctor and his expression wasn't too hopeful when I asked if you could play after you recovered."

"What do you mean? I thought I just had to wait three months! You said I just had to recover," exclaimed Sarah.

"I know, but your doctor said there is a possibility of permanent damage which means you may never be able to play again."

Sarah sat in complete silence, staring out of the window in her hospital room. The color had left her face and she looked as if she had seen a ghost. She contemplated her loss and what this meant for her future as Miranda tried to console her. Sarah wondered what this would do to her. She had lost her dream, her life, and her purpose in one fell swoop. Her mind swarmed with thoughts such as what would she do now? How would she live her life? What would she do in her spare time? What did she have if not soccer?

"Meer, I need to be alone now. I'll call you if I need you, until then I think I need to take some time for myself."

"Okay. Make sure to let me know if you need anything, Sarah. You know I'm here for you."

Sarah spent the next month in agony over her disability and her rehab. It was difficult for her. It was hard for her to walk, run, or to even pick her legs up properly. However, she knew she had to get through it for her sister's sake. The recovery process was long and tiresome. Sarah needed assistance with simple tasks such as: using the restroom, lying in bed, and even eating sometimes. Since Sarah had asked for time to herself, she had more opportunity to consider all of her options. She thought about the state she was in and how her condition would affect her position in the long run. After much deliberation, she decided she would strive for a new goal in life: she wanted to live her life. She wanted to go outside to breathe the fresh air of the city. She wanted to feel free. Sarah knew that even if things would never be the same for her again, she needed to be free. Free to make her own decisions and follow her own path rather than devoting herself to one thing and one thing alone. Her freedom was in the clouds and the fresh air. It was in the warm summer and the winter chills. She decided to never take the little things for granted ever again.

It was April 12th. Sarah had completed her rehab and did an outstanding job on her physical examinations. April 12th was the day that she was able to go outside for the first time in a long time. Sarah Yameen felt the wind in her hair and the strands dance about in delight. She viewed the world with a different perspective now. She took it all in, the flowers, the blades of grass, and even the dirt road. It was all so beautiful to her. She looked up to the sky and watched as birds flew past and she also felt like she was soaring right alongside them. She felt as if there was nothing holding her back anymore. She was free.

I AM IN CONTROL

Khadidiatou Thiam

I heard the wind whistling.
It's like I'm hearing my name.
I'll follow the noise,
If it gets me in trouble I'm the one to blame.
As I listen to the tunes,
I get a feeling of regret.
Something telling me I'm not ready for what's next.
But I still follow the noise
And it leads me to big trees
With leaves as blue as the sea.
There's a sign to the left saying don't pick off a leaf.
But I take it anyways because I do as I please.

FREEDOM OF RELIGION

Shajida Begum

Aashiyana didn't believe in religion, not even as a child. Religions, like Islam, never made sense to her. However, she used to believe in Allah, the almighty god who created the world. After all, she was like most Muslim children. It was drilled in her head that there is no god except for Allah and the prophet Muhammad is Allah's only messenger. Her mesab, or Muslim teacher, told her to write there is no god except Allah, every day, every time, and to learn this in her heart. There is no way she could doubt or deny the existence of the all-powerful omnipotent and omnipresent Allah.

As a child, she doubted and questioned herself when she used to read bronze age moral stories in the Quran and other Islamic books. She used to quickly reassure herself by saying that religion may be made by people, but Allah was real. There must be a god called Allah. Her mom and mesab used to scold her every time she used to doubt and ask a question about religion. Her mom and mesab used to warn her not to use the Devil's thinking and skills, that Allah is testing her faith and that she should feel guilty for doubting the existence of the all-powerful Allah. Her mom constantly used to threaten her about Satan and eternal hell fire if she didn't behave like a pious, modest Muslim girl. She could not sleep at night because she literally wanted to believe in the existence of Allah and things, such as the angel Gabriel. Instead believed in other superstitious, unethical characters.

Between ages six to ten she was extremely superstitious. She used to have her mom hang images of Arabic writing in the living room, bedroom, and everywhere in the house. She used to feel guilty every time she used to stretch her legs while lying down on a sofa and her legs used to point toward Arabic writings that mentioned Allah's name. She used to feel as if she were pointing her legs to God. She used to feel guilty if she accidentally put her science book on top of her Islamic books. She believed that the Qur'an and other Islamic books were and should always be placed above mere science books.

In fact, all the furniture in her house, and in most Muslim houses, is arranged in a way so that your feet never point towards the Kaaba in Mecca. After coming home from school, she used to watch Islamic movies. She lived her childhood and teenage life with fear in her heart. However, she was also exposed to history and her family was much more religious compared to the average Bengali or Pakistani family. Her parents enrolled her in the most expensive high school in Bangladesh. Unlike her mother, her father hadn't forced religion, the hijab, or the Abaya down her throat. Her father actually gave her more freedom than was ever granted to an average Bengali Muslim girl. However, everything slowly started to change as she grew up. Both her parents told her that she should no longer study and that she should drop out of high school. When she was in kindergarden, her dad used to constantly taunt her about her high tuition fees and threatened to pull her out of school. She never thought that would actually happen though. Her peers were not allowed to go to school and instead were forced into arranged marriages. When she turned sixteen, her parents no longer wanted her to go to school either.

The Bangladeshi government was very strict as well. They were notoriously famous for banning websites such as YouTube and Facebook and even the whole internet because the internet contains atheist bloggers, cartoons, and other anti-Islamic content. She used to be very angry at her government for shutting down social media because of anti-Islamic videos.

She was raised in a conservative society and she was always taught that religion is the holiest thing and more important than critical thought. Yet, she deeply believed that you must respect others' beliefs even if they have no religion. She folded her sleeves and aggressively logged into Facebook to give a piece of her mind to the people insulting her birth religion, Islam. She encountered an atheist on a random anti-Islam account who spoke very rudely to her and opened her eyes.

The last time she read a Qur'an was when she was in seventh grade, but even during that grade she could not take religion and outdated verses seriously. However, she still firmly believed that religion should be respected and Allah did exist. She kept making excuses but went back to reading the Qur'an again for the first time after becoming an adult. She dug deeply for truth and did her own homework and research. She was also taking her exams during that time though and she studied evolution for the first time in her life.

She was agnostic from 2017 until April 2018 and then she fully came out as an atheist on 2018. Initially, she called herself agnostic because she just could not give up the idea of an all-powerful creator. Later, she realized that the silly, sadistic gods described in the scripture could not exist in reality like the Islamic preachers' speeches said, or like those of Zakir Naik's, and Islamic movies. Her friends' forced marriages, her parents' refusal to educate her and their desire to marry her off, and numerous terrorist attacks and gross atrocities committed in the name of Islam forced her to seriously question her birth religion and culture more.

She read the Quran and Hadith again and she found out that it contradicted her particular upbringing and scientific education that she had received at her private English high school. She first heard about the term atheist in 2018 and finally she found a label that suited her well. She became more confident and independent after becoming an atheist. She stopped believing in a supernatural power and took complete charge of her life. She was able to stand up against a forced arranged marriage and she demanded her right to receive an education. In the end, she found that atheism truly freed her from the shackles of Islam.

Freedom is different for different people. Freedom is just freedom though and although freedom is freedom, everyone doesn’t have an equal amount.

- Ta'lasha Hilton

THE SPOON

Tisha Islam

Clutter. Clutter. My hands start trembling. I don't feel anything but numbness from my lower hips to my arms. I constantly lose my balance as I sit on this wooden chair and my head feels too heavy for my body. My arms fail to stretch forward once again and reach and grasp the one thing that I want more than the sticker I saw on Mr. Talk-A-Lot's desk yesterday. That's my science teacher, by the way. His actual name is Mr. Wilde and he does, indeed, talk *a lot*. That's not the point right now, though.

Sitting on this kitchen table, you would think I would dive right into the food. I mean I am really hungry. Mom made turkey salad and spinach noodles for lunch and she said it was especially for me. I'm lucky, in a way, since I have no siblings. I don't really have to fight to get anything. That most definitely includes food. I only know this because my best friend, Andrew, told me he stole some Cheez-Its from his brother's room and in return ended up getting scratches on his cheeks. Yes, they fought over Cheez-Its. But I call myself lucky in that case, and Dad is always at work so the food stays for my tummy only. The doctor said since it's hard for me to chew and eat though, I should stick to high quality food that helps me meet my nutritional requirements. Since then, I've just gotten used to eating leafy greens and food like salads.

Last time I had actual yummy food was the lasagna mom fed me two days ago. The breakfast at school this morning wasn't the best either. Andrew poured the milk in my cereal for me, but it ended up spilling everywhere because I knocked it over with my arm. I tried the little bit that was left but the milk just tasted disgusting and spoiled-

"Noah dear, you have to try and hurry up because you have an appointment with Dr. Mills soon," Mom yells from her room upstairs. Dr. Mills is my physical therapist. He's helped me through a lot over the last few years. He's a close friend of Dad's too.

"Alri-ri..ght..Mom. I'll try to hurry," I respond.

"Baby, if you need me to come down and help you get that food in your belly, please, let me know. Don't be stubborn," Mom says. I'm *not* being stubborn. I just want to try it myself for once, like other normal kids, and eat with my own two hands. Of course, no one would understand. They just think I'm a little weakling. I don't want to tell Mom that, though.

My plate is still full. Once again, I try to grasp the spoon that lies on the side of my plate. I see that it's right there but somehow when I try to reach it again, my hand just slips right off. Another fail. I'm just really hungry but I can't get myself to pick up this darn spoon. "Mom, I-I..I might...need your...your help," I say.

Mom rushes down the stairs and comes to the kitchen. "Here, honey. Open wide, c'mon, we have to get going," she says as she sits beside me and picks up the spoon. I look at her getting almost teary-eyed.

"Mom...do you-you think...I can...be normal- ever?" I ask her.

"Oh, sweetie, don't say that. This isn't something you can control. Think of it this way: You've been fighting this monster, Cerebral Palsy, since you were born. That would be like eleven years now, right? You're definitely an uncommon case. And you, my dear, also can't be normal because you are extra extra extraordinary," she replies.

It's hard to believe what she was saying. "But...but, look. You have to feed me still. I thought...I-I could use my own hand. I can't walk, t-talk, or even...eat normal-ly."

"You are my strong boy and, soon enough, you'll get even stronger. For that though, you need to hurry and chomp chomp so we can get done with your physical therapy. But son, me, your dad, Dr. Mills, and everyone else are all here for you."

I give a little nod and a half smile.

After I get done eating, we head to Dr. Mills. He already checked with all the patients in his office. I was just the last one. As we wait patiently, I see this one boy across from us laughing so cheerfully as he struggles to walk. His legs look like those of robots and he looks like he's my age-

"Hey guys, today's appointment was just for a regular checkup. Noah's next session will be Thursday of next week. From last week we have seen some improvement with him. He's in need of the wheelchair less from better walking skills. However, his bones are still weak and muscles still lack strength. We may need another two or three months of continuous sessions until he's back on track with that," Dr. Mills explains.

It's not the same when you're binded by some things. This just feels different.

"Here, Noah. This might help you to cheer up. My wife made this cheesecake and I thought I'd save some for you since you were coming," Dr. Mills said as he hands me a small plate and a spoon.

Mom reaches out to grab the spoon, but I slowly shift my body in the other direction. "I got it," I say. She looks at me as if I might knock off the whole plate. I look down at the plate and spoon, then look back up at their expecting glances. Slowly, slowly, I extend my arm to reach the bottom of that utensil. Oh no, my hands are shaking again. I feel myself losing balance even though I'm sitting still. No, I got *this.* Inch by inch, I get closer to the spoon. Once I feel a touch, I tighten my grip on it. I turn my head and look at Mom with a grin from ear to ear. Then shaking and slow, I bring the spoon closer to my mouth.

Mom and Dr. Mills's mouths opened wide. Their expressions dropped from eagerness to ecstasy. Both looked at me with proud eyes and delighted smiles. "Did it, Mom. I-I...did it!" Even through the stutters, saying those words never made me feel more content in my life.

We have to make ourselves give us freedom instead of listening to others.

- Shelby Parham

UNCAGED

Ke'ir Woodfolk

I beat my captors that tried to rip me like raptors.
I outsmarted their weak without any leaks.
I burst through the cage, though I am not a mage.
Through the blast, I am free at last.
As I continue to fly to avoid the great lies.
Going through lanes and seeing back more of my days.
This isn't meant to be staged, as I remain....uncaged.

EXEMPTION

Saif Miah

Like a dog without a leash
Not getting held back with defeat
Considering the rights I deserve
Making choice with determination I preserve

Not made with lightness on my tongue
With new hopes and ambitions that have sprung
I step aside from evil, hatred, and attention
This mind doesn't eat any apprehension

I swear I won't quiet down
And in words my opinions have no frown
No matter if society stands for the poor and weakened
I'll stand alone in this world which I speak in.

IT'S MY TURN

Jaima Rahman

A mind of my own
A heart, my will's throne
Considering what I've been taught
Finding the answers I sought

I shut my ears to the world
I walk my own path, no longer just a girl
I've reached my peak
And found the answers that I seek

Hatred shouts at me
I shun the menaces of society
Manipulate me no more
Nothing but strength deep down to my core

Let me talk my talk
For it is my own path that I walk
It's time to listen, my determined voice
My life
My choice

MY DAY WITH LANI

Catherine Stewart

I Woke Up Grateful To See Another Day.
I Take A Shower.
Eat Breakfast And Call My Dearest Friend.
Lani Said She Was Ready For Our Day To Begin.
First We Went To Get Ice Cream .
After That We Walked Down The River Side.
Later In The Day We Ate Dinner.
We Went To An Italian Restaurant.
She Got Whatever She Wanted .
Next I Took Her Home.
I Walked Her To The Door Kissed Her Forehead.
Then I Said Goodnight.
When I Got Home I Thought About Her Until I Fell Asleep.
Oh How Much I Love Lani.

WHAT IS FREEDOM?

Shanice Bass

Is it being able to do what you want?
Is it just having fun?
Being able to make your own choices?
Is it being able to say you can't?
Or being able to talk to whomever you want?
Is it being whomever you want?

Is it choosing your curfew & bedtime?
Being able to make your own money?
Is it expressing thoughts & opinions?
Is it being able to forget my past?
How do you know you are free?
How do you know you will always have your freedom?

What in the world is freedom?
Freedom is independence.
Freedom is empowerment.
Freedom is self- government.
Freedom is entitlement.
Freedom is what you make it.
It is not a privilege, it is earned

Freedom to me is being able to be myself. Sure, there are many ways people could be free; you can be free to use your phone, be free from jail, or even be free from a relationship. A lot of people think that being free is being able to do what you want, which I agree with. But for me, it's also a spiritual thing. People should have the freedom to be who they want and think the way they want to think: freedom to be themselves.

- Anissa Duynslager

WORKS CITED

"America's Sex Education: How We Are Failing Our Students." Blog, 18 Sept. 2017, nursing.usc.edu/blog/americas-sex-education/.

"Sexuality Education." *Advocates for Youth*, advocatesforyouth.org/resources/fact-sheets/sexuality-education-2/.

"Should College Be Free? Here's What You Need to Consider." *Trade*, www.trade-schools.net/articles/should-college-be-free.asp

"Why Should Colleges Be Free? Pros And Cons Of Tuition-Free College." *College Raptor Blog*, www.collegeraptor.com/find-colleges/articles/affordability-college-cost/pros-cons-tuition-free-college/.

www.ingramcontent.com/pod-product-compliance
Lightning Source LLC
Chambersburg PA
CBHW021621030826
48979CB00035B/1492/J

* 9 7 8 0 3 5 9 6 7 3 5 1 3 *